Happy Birthday,
BIG BAD WOLF

Frank Asch

XZ
A

KIDS CAN PRESS

Kids Can Press acknowledges the financial support of the Government of Ontario, through the Ontario Media Development Corporation's Ontario Book Initiative.

Published in Canada by
Kids Can Press Ltd.
25 Dockside Drive
Toronto, ON M5A 0B5

Published in the U.S. by
Kids Can Press Ltd.
2250 Military Road
Tonawanda, NY 14150

www.kidscanpress.com

Kids Can Press is a *Corus*™ Entertainment company

The artwork in this book was rendered in Photoshop. The text is set in Providence Sans Bold.

Edited by Tara Walker
Designed by Karen Powers

This book is smyth sewn casebound.
Manufactured in Singapore in 10/2010
by Tien Wah Press (Pte) Ltd.

CM 11 0 9 8 7 6 5 4 3 2 1

Library and Archives Canada Cataloguing in Publication

Asch, Frank
    Happy birthday, big bad wolf / Frank Asch.

ISBN 978-1-55337-368-1

1. Wolves—Juvenile fiction. 2. Swine—Juvenile fiction.
I. Title.

PZ7.A778Ha 2011   j813'.54   C2010-904763-X

The Pig family — Poppa Pig, Momma Pig and Little Pig — were enjoying a quiet afternoon when suddenly there was a loud knock on the door.

"Oh my!" said Momma Pig as she peeked out from behind the curtain. "It's the Big Bad Wolf!"

"Quick, everyone hide!" whispered Poppa Pig,
and the Pig family ducked behind the sofa.

Remembering his grandfather's surprise party, Little Pig thought, "Oh, it must be the Big Bad Wolf's birthday."

So when the front door flew open and the Big Bad Wolf stomped into the house, Little Pig jumped out from behind the sofa and shouted, "Surprise!"

"Oh no!" whispered Momma Pig to Poppa Pig.
"Little Pig thinks it's the Big Bad Wolf's birthday.
What should we do?"

"The only thing we can do," said Poppa Pig.
"Go along with it."

So Momma and Poppa Pig jumped
up from behind the sofa and shouted,

"Happy Birthday, Big Bad Wolf!"

"You pigs are crazy," growled the Big Bad Wolf. "My birthday was weeks ago."

"Oh, sorry," said Poppa Pig with a nervous grin. "We were ... uh ... too busy to throw you a birthday party then. But we were hoping this would do. You know what they say: better late than never!"

"Throw me a party?" said the Big Bad Wolf. "No one ever threw me a birthday party before!"

"There's a first time for everything," replied Momma Pig. "What kind of birthday cake would you like? Chocolate or vanilla?"

"Pick the chocolate," said Little Pig as he licked his lips. "That's the best!"

"Okay, chocolate it is!" cried Momma Pig. "Wait here. We'll be right back!"

"Hmmm ... Pigs for dinner and cake for dessert," thought the Big Bad Wolf. "That sounds just fine to me."

Once they were in the kitchen, Momma Pig whispered to Poppa Pig, "This is terrible! We can't fool the Big Bad Wolf forever!"

"Don't worry," Poppa Pig whispered back. "We'll just stall until nighttime comes. Then we'll sneak outside and hide in the forest. He'll never find us in the dark."

While the Big Bad Wolf waited for his birthday cake to bake, Little Pig went into his room and opened his toy box. "The Big Bad Wolf ought to have a present," he thought and selected a toy of his own to wrap in pretty paper.

"What's that?" asked the Big Bad Wolf as Little Pig
returned with the pretty package.
"This is your present," said Little Pig.

"Gosh, I never got a birthday present before," said the Big Bad Wolf as he unwrapped his gift.

It was a snuggle bunny. But the Big Bad Wolf didn't know that. He thought it might be something to eat.

"Silly wolf!" cried Little Pig. "You don't EAT snuggle toys. You snuggle them!"

By now it was getting dark outside. As Momma Pig brought in the birthday cake, Poppa Pig turned off the lights and everyone sang "Happy Birthday" to the Big Bad Wolf.

"Now we EAT!" declared the Big Bad Wolf.

"Wait!" cried Little Pig. "First you have to make a secret wish and blow out your candles!"

"Right," said the Big Bad Wolf, and he wished the Pig family hadn't been so nice to him.

Then he huffed and he puffed and he not only blew out the candles, he blew the candles right off the cake!

All of a sudden it was dark in the Pig family's
house. While the Big Bad Wolf searched for the light
switch, Poppa and Momma Pig scooped up Little Pig
and ran out the door.

"Where are we going?" asked Little Pig.

"Shhhh!" said Poppa Pig as he carried him into the forest.

"Safe at last!" cried Momma Pig.

Finally the Big Bad Wolf found the light switch and discovered that he was all by himself.

"Where did everyone go?" he cried. "And what about my birthday?"

Suddenly he realized that he had been tricked. First he felt angry. Then he felt hurt.

"I'm all alone on my birthday!" he howled as big warm tears gushed out his eyes and ran down his nose.

"Poor Big Bad Wolf," thought Little Pig, and he bolted from his father's arms.

"No! Wait! Come back!" cried Momma and Poppa Pig.

But it was too late.

Little Pig ran into the house and gave the Big Bad Wolf a great big hug. "Don't cry," he said. "You're not alone. I'm right here by your side."

Momma and Poppa Pig had no choice but to follow
Little Pig back home.

"Why did you leave me all alone?" whimpered the Big Bad Wolf.

"Um ... We were just playing hide-and-seek," explained Poppa Pig.

"That's right," said Momma Pig. "Birthday parties always have
games, don't they?"

"I guess so," replied the Big Bad Wolf with a sniffle.

Little Pig ran and got the Big Bad Wolf a tissue. "Here, blow your nose!" he said.

"But not too hard," said Poppa Pig. "We don't want you knocking over any furniture."

Then the Pig family played pin-the-tail-on-the-donkey, sit-on-the-balloon and musical chairs with the Big Bad Wolf.

After the games Little Pig said, "Hey, we forgot to eat the Big Bad Wolf's birthday cake! Shouldn't we eat it now?"

"Not until we've all had some supper," said Poppa Pig.

The Big Bad Wolf's ears perked up. As much as he liked the taste of pork, there was no way he could eat the Pig family now. But he was still hungry.

"Supper?" he asked.

"Yes, supper," replied Momma Pig, and she set out a fine spread of soup and salad and vegetable casserole.

"This is dee-licious!" announced the Big Bad Wolf.

"But the best part is yet to come," said Little Pig.

And they all had a big piece of the Big Bad Wolf's chocolate birthday cake.

"This has been the best birthday of my entire life!" declared the Big Bad Wolf. "But it's getting late now and I have to go home."

"Why don't you stay over?" asked Poppa Pig.

"We have room on our couch," added Momma Pig.

"I wouldn't want to impose," replied the Big Bad Wolf.

"Please," pleaded Little Pig.

"Well ... all right!" agreed the Big Bad Wolf.

While Momma Pig fixed up the couch with blankets and a soft pillow, Little Pig went into his bedroom to put on his pajamas. When he came out to say goodnight, the Big Bad Wolf was already fast asleep snuggled up close to his new bunny.

"Happy Birthday, Big Bad Wolf," Little Pig whispered.